THE ISLE of STRUAY

Grannie's

The Mainland

The Jetty

ISLE of STRUAY
SHOP & POST OFFICE

OBAN TIMES
GET YOUR COPY HERE

The Shop & Post Office

ALSO BY MAIRI HEDDERWICK

Katie Morag and the Big Boy Cousins
Katie Morag and the Tiresome Ted
Katie Morag and the Two Grandmothers
Katie Morag and the New Pier

To all small places

A Red Fox Book. Published by Random House Children's Books
20 Vauxhall Bridge Road, London SW1V 2SA

First published in 1984 by The Bodley Head Children's Books
First published in paperback by Picture Lions 1986
Red Fox edition 1994

RANDOM HOUSE UK Limited Reg. No. 954009

ISBN 0 09 911861 0

KATIE MORAG DELIVERS THE MAIL

High Farm

The Holiday House

Mrs Bayview's

The Lady A

The Redburn Bridge

The Village

KATIE MORAG DELIVERS THE MAIL

Mairi Hedderwick

RED FOX

Wednesdays were always hectic on the Isle of Struay, for that was the day that the boat brought mail and provisions from the mainland.

One particular Wednesday was worse than usual, since baby Liam was cutting his first tooth and both Mr and Mrs McColl were in a bad mood.

"All right, all right," said Mrs McColl in exasperation. "I'll take Liam upstairs to quieten him down! Katie Morag, you take the mail to the houses across the Bay. There are five parcels—one for each house. The one with the red label is for Grannie."

Pleased to escape, Katie Morag set off. She loved any excuse to visit her Grannie, who lived all alone in the very last house on the other side of the Bay.

But it was a hot day, and Katie Morag had just stopped for a moment to paddle in a pool beneath the Redburn Bridge, when suddenly—*splash!*—she slipped on a slithery stone and fell into the water, mailbag and all.

"Oh, dear! Oh, dear!" wailed Katie Morag, looking at the five soggy
parcels. "All the addresses are smudged and I won't know which parcel is for
which house now!"

Only Grannie's parcel was still recognizable by its red label.

Then, because she was so frightened and ashamed, Katie Morag did a silly thing. She ran the rest of the way to the other side of the Bay and threw a

parcel—any parcel, except the red-labelled one—on to the doorstep of each of
the first four houses. Nobody saw her. Still sobbing, she ran on to Grannie's.

"Well, this is a fine *boorach* you've got yourself into, Katie Morag," said Grannie, when Katie Morag had explained what she had done. "Still at least you've given *me* the right parcel—it's got the spare part for the tractor that I've been waiting for. I'll go and get the old grey lady going, while you dry yourself up. Then you can try and sort the whole muddle out."

Grannie had her head under the bonnet of the tractor for a long time.
Occasionally, Katie Morag heard muffled words of anger and she thought of
the angry words waiting for her at home . . .

Then, suddenly, with a cough of black smoke, the tractor stuttered into life
and they set off to go round each of the four houses in turn.

The first house belonged to the Lady Artist. She had been expecting tiny, thin brushes for her miniature paintings, but the parcel Katie Morag had left on her doorstep contained two enormous brushes.

"They're bigger than my painting boards!" she said in disgust.

The second house was rented by the Holiday People. They had ordered
fishing hooks from a sports catalogue, but their parcel had been full of garden
seeds.

"We can't catch fish with daisies and lettuces!" they complained.

At the third house, Mr MacMaster was standing by a big barrel of whitewash, holding the Lady Artist's paint brushes.

"How can I paint my walls with these fiddling little things?" he asked.

In the fourth house lived Mrs Bayview. "That stupid shop on the mainland!
Where are my seeds? Flowers won't grow out of *these*," she said crossly,
waving a packet of fishing hooks in the air.

After much trundling back and forth, Katie Morag finally managed to
collect and deliver all the right things to all the right people.
Everyone smiled and waved and said, "Thank you very much."

By now it was getting dark. Katie Morag thought of the long journey home.
She would be very late and her parents were so bad-tempered these days on
account of Liam's noisy teething.

"Grannie, would you like to come back for tea?" she asked.

Katie Morag half hid behind Grannie as they walked in the kitchen door but, to her surprise, everyone was smiling. Liam had cut his tooth at last and all was calm.

"Thank you for helping out today, Katie Morag," said Mrs McColl. "Isn't she good, Grannie?"

"Och aye," said Grannie with a smile as she looked at Katie Morag. "She's very good at sorting things out, is our Katie Morag." And she said no more.

Some
bestselling Red Fox
picture books

THE BIG ALFIE AND ANNIE ROSE STORYBOOK
by Shirley Hughes
OLD BEAR
by Jane Hissey
OI! GET OFF OUR TRAIN
by John Burningham
DON'T DO THAT!
by Tony Ross
NOT NOW, BERNARD
by David McKee
ALL JOIN IN
by Quentin Blake
THE WHALES' SONG
by Gary Blythe and Dyan Sheldon
JESUS' CHRISTMAS PARTY
by Nicholas Allan
THE PATCHWORK CAT
by Nicola Bayley and William Mayne
MATILDA
by Hilaire Belloc and Posy Simmonds
WILLY AND HUGH
by Anthony Browne
THE WINTER HEDGEHOG
by Ann and Reg Cartwright
A DARK, DARK TALE
by Ruth Brown
HARRY, THE DIRTY DOG
by Gene Zion and Margaret Bloy Graham
DR XARGLE'S BOOK OF EARTHLETS
by Jeanne Willis and Tony Ross
WHERE'S THE BABY?
by Pat Hutchins